To the Lovitt family
and their newest Little Pip, Keely Grace.
She's a good egg!
– KW

For Isaac and Daniel
– JC

SIMON AND SCHUSTER
First published in Great Britain in 2010 by Simon and Schuster UK Ltd
1st Floor, 222 Gray's Inn Road, London, WC1X 8HB
A CBS Company

Originally published in 2010 by Margaret K. McElderry Books,
an imprint of Simon and Schuster Children's Publishing Division, New York

A CIP catalogue record for this book is available from the British Library upon request

ISBN: 978 1 84738 822 3

Printed in China

10 9 8 7 6 5 4 3 2 1

What's in the Egg, Little Pip?

Karma Wilson illustrated by Jane Chapman

SIMON AND SCHUSTER
London   New York   Sydney

Little Pip stared at the Egg.
The large, white oval rested on Mummy's
feet just under her soft, warm belly. Pip used
to sleep there, but there was no room for her
now, not since the Egg. Mummy and Daddy
asked, "What do you think, Little Pip?"

Pip shrugged. She wasn't sure.

Mummy and Daddy had talked about the Egg for a long time.
Yesterday morning they had woken Pip and said,
"The Egg is finally here, Little Pip!"
And they sang. . .

"The Egg, the Egg, the lovely Egg,
a wonderful, glorious sight.
A sister or brother for sweet Little Pip
will soon make our family just right."

Pip frowned. The Egg didn't look like much of sister or brother.

"Our family is just right," Pip said. "That Egg can't make it better."

Mummy nuzzled Pip and said, "Just wait. You may be surprised. And now, Daddy, it's time for you to take over."

Mummy carefully nudged the Egg and tucked it on Daddy's feet. Then Daddy nestled down onto the Egg.

"Where are you going, Mummy?" Pip asked.

"I need to go and fish for food," Mummy said, "but somebody must always be with the Egg to keep it warm. So Daddy will watch the Egg while I fish, and I will watch the Egg when Daddy fishes."

"Can I go with you?" Pip pleaded.

Mummy smiled and shook her head. "You stay and
help Daddy keep the Egg warm and safe.

Pip sighed. "I'm too little to help. I'm still your baby."

Mummy shook her head. "You have grown up so
much, Little Pip. You're big enough to help Daddy.
You're even big enough to help the Egg!
But don't worry, you will always be our baby."

Pip wasn't so sure. As she watched Mummy
waddle away, a tear slipped down her
cheek. Now it was just her and Daddy . . .
and the Egg.

Later that day Pip chirped,
"Daddy, let's slide on the ice."

Daddy shook his head.
"I can't leave the Egg, Little Pip."

Pip frowned.
"Not even for a minute?"

"Not even for a second," Daddy smiled.
"That's what families do, Little Pip.
I did the same for you when you
were just an egg."

Pip couldn't imagine that she was ever just an egg.
Why had Mummy and Daddy even wanted the Egg?
I should be enough! thought Pip.
She wandered off to think, and as
she slumped along she sang,

"The Egg, the Egg, it's all the Egg.
Nobody cares about me.
I liked it best before the Egg,
back when our family was three."

Little Pip felt all alone so she decided to look for
her best friend, Merry. "Do you want to go and slide?" she asked.

"I suppose so," said Merry. She didn't seem her usual cheerful self.
"Does your family have an egg too?" asked Pip.

Merry nodded and stamped her foot. "I don't see what all the fuss
is about. The egg just sits there and does nothing."

"I know," said Pip. "But it's all Mummy and Daddy talk about or think about anymore. I want to forget about the Eggs. Let's slide!"

And so they did.

WHOOP!

WHEEE!

WHISH!

They didn't think about the Eggs again.

But suddenly the sun disappeared
behind a thick, black cloud.

"A storm!" squealed Pip.
"We must run! **Hurry!**"

"We're too little," said Merry. "We can't!"

Pip ruffled her feathers and puffed out her chest. "My mummy said I'm big enough to help the Egg. We have to go and help. RUN!"

They raced the stormcloud all the way home.

Just as they reached home, frozen sleet started to fall
in cold, stinging drops. Pip snuggled tight against
her Daddy, helping to shield the Egg.

There they huddled, and there they waited.

And waited.

And waited.

Finally Mummy returned. Pip's tummy growled.
She was glad to eat the fish Mummy had brought back for them.
But then Daddy had to go fishing.

Storms came and went, and the Egg always had to be kept warm. Pip, Mummy, and Daddy huddled around the Egg for many weeks. Sometimes Mummy left to fish, sometimes Daddy did, but Pip always stayed with the Egg.

Then one bright, sunny day, while Mummy was away fishing . . .

CHIP,
CHIP,
CRACK.

"The Egg is broken, Daddy!" Pip cried, and buried her head into Daddy's chest. All that work, for nothing.

Craaaaaack.

Pip gasped. The Egg was gone.
In its place sat a beautiful penguin chick.

"It's a chick! A chick, Daddy!"

"Little Pip, meet your brother."

At the beach lots of penguins were squawking
and talking. Pip saw a flock of penguins
just back from fishing. Mummy was home!

Mummy sighed with happiness. "He looks just
like you when you were a baby, Pip!"

Pip smiled. "I was that small?"

"Oh yes," said Mummy. "Just that small."

Pip looked at her new brother and she sang,

"Welcome, chick, you lovely chick.
What a wonderful, glorious sight.
Little brother, I name you Sam.
You make our family just right."

Little Pip looked around and saw all the penguin families
snuggling new chicks in their pebbly nests. Pip waved
to Merry and Merry waved back, a huge smile on her face.

Pip smiled too.
Everything felt
just right.